Dedication

This book is dedicated in loving memory of Marcus, Shawn, little Danny and baby Anthony - gone too soon but never forgotten.

MINDSTIR MEDIA

Juju went to the park to meet his best friends Scooter and Jewels. Right away, his friends saw that something was wrong with Juju. He was not his energetic happy self and he wore a big confused frown on his face.

Jewels was the first to speak. "Hi Juju! Where is Auggie and Izzy?" Jewels was ready to play Frisbee.

Juju sat down on the bench and said nothing. "Why are you sad Juju?" asked Scooter.

He thought maybe something happened to Juju's baby brother and sister.

Juju said to his friends, "my mommy is sick."

"Does she have a cold?" asked Jewels.

"No," said Juju, "she has breast cancer."

Scooter and Jewels looked at each other. They didn't know what to say.

"It's all my fault. Mommy asked me to help around the house and I told her I didn't want to!

If I would have pitched in, she wouldn't be sick," Juju said.

Juju began to explain to his friends. "Mommy went to her doctor and that's how they found the cancer.

She has to go to the hospital and have an operation to get the cancer out."

Scooter and Jewels looked at each other.
This was definitely not just a cold.

Jewels tried to reassure Juju.

She had a family member that had breast cancer.

She said, "I wouldn't worry. My auntie had breast cancer, and she is doing just fine." That made Juju feel a little better, but not much.

There would be no playing Frisbee today.

"She will lose all of her hair when they put the medicine in her," said Juju. Jewels replied, "It's special medicine, and it helps to keep the cancer gone." "Will her hair grow back?" asked Juju. Jewels explained, "Of course it will! And it will grow back even softer."

Then Scooter added, "I know what we can do, we can be there for your Mommy and help her!"

Juju loved this idea.

Jewels, Scooter and Juju began talking about ways they could help.

The next day, Jewels and Scooter went to Juju's house. They had a plan to help his Mommy.

Mommy came downstairs and saw the gang in the living room. Jewels and Scooter said hello.

"What are you all up to?" asked Mommy.

Juju replied, "we want to help. I'm sorry you are sick." Mommy smiled at them.

Juju took his Mommy's hand and led her to her favorite chair.

"What color would you like for your nails?"

"I have petunia pink, outrageous orange and rock-a-bye red." said Jewels. Mommy laughed, "I choose petunia pink."

Jewels began painting her fingernails.

Juju was in his room cleaning up.

Mommy walked in and looked very surprised.

"Mommy," said Juju, "look at the good job I did cleaning my room."

"Maybe if I had cleaned my room more, you wouldn't be sick," he said sadly.

Mommy said to Juju, "sometimes people get sick and they also get better. There was nothing you did to make me sick."

"I want you to know you can always come to me and Daddy if you have any questions or just want to talk, okay?"

Juju nodded.

In the kitchen, Scooter and Jewels made breakfast.

They knew breakfast was the most important meal of the day.

"I see you made breakfast for me," said Mommy.

"This has been a good day! I feel better already!"

They all smiled, their plan worked.

Then Mommy said, "why don't you kids go outside now and play Frisbee?"

CPSIA information can be obtained
at www.ICGtesting.com
Printed in the USA
LVHW071023150920
665888LV00008B/2

9 780099 735751 6